BLAZERS

CRIME SOLVERS

LOOKING FOR
FINGERPRINTS

by Melissa Langley Biegert

Consultant:
David Foran, PhD
Director, Forensic Science Program
Michigan State University

Reading Consultant:
Barbara J. Fox
Reading Specialist
North Carolina State University

Capstone
press

Mankato, Minnesota

Blazers is published by Capstone Press,
151 Good Counsel Drive, P.O. Box 669, Mankato, Minnesota 56002.
www.capstonepress.com

 Books published by Capstone Press are manufactured with paper
containing at least 10 percent post-consumer waste.

Library of Congress Cataloging-in-Publication Data
Biegert, Melissa Ann Langley, 1967–
    Looking for fingerprints / by Melissa Langley Biegert.
    p. cm. — (Blazers. Crime solvers)
    Includes bibliographical references and index.
    Summary: "Describes methods used by experts to find and examine fingerprint evidence to
solve crimes" — Provided by publisher.
    ISBN 978-1-4296-3372-7 (library binding)
    1. Fingerprints — Juvenile literature. 2. Criminal investigation — Juvenile literature. I. Title.
II. Series.
HV6074.B46 2010
363.25'8 — dc22   2009014607

Editorial Credits
Megan Schoeneberger, editor; Matt Bruning, designer; Eric Gohl, media researcher

Photo Credits
Alamy/Beate Rud, 11; Stuart Walker, 14
AP Images, 18; Heribert Proepper, 21; Pacific Daily News, Masako Watanabe, 15; Toby Talbot, 24
Art Life Images/Paco Ayala, 27
Capstone Press/Karon Dubke, badge (all), cover (all), 5, 6, 9, 10, 13, 17 (tabletop, tweezers),
    22–23, 29 (top), 30
Courtesy of Dr. David Foran, Michigan State University, 17 (top right, top left), 19 (all, except
    top left and top middle)
iStockphoto/Hans Laubel, 25
Photolibrary/Jochen Tack, 28
Shutterstock, 12; arfo, fingerprint (design element), 17 (middle), 19 (top middle); AVAVA, 16;
    ene, 26; Kevin L Chesson, 22 (computer screen); Loren Rodgers, 8; Neo Edmund, handprint
    (design element); PeJo, 29 (bottom); pzAxe, 19 (top left); Spauln, 4

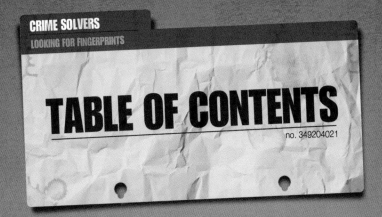

CRIME SOLVERS
LOOKING FOR FINGERPRINTS

TABLE OF CONTENTS

no. 349204021

CHAPTER ONE

THE HIDDEN CLUES

Someone's house has been robbed!
Jewelry, cash, and TVs are missing. But
the **criminals** left behind few clues.

criminal – someone who commits a crime

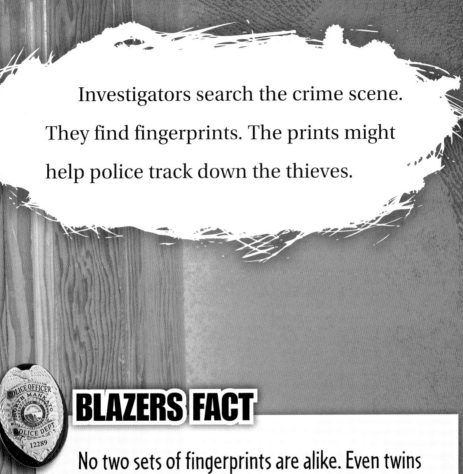

Investigators search the crime scene. They find fingerprints. The prints might help police track down the thieves.

BLAZERS FACT

No two sets of fingerprints are alike. Even twins do not have matching prints.

CHAPTER TWO

ON THE SCENE

Some prints at a crime scene are easy to see. **Patent** fingerprints are often left by a person with dirty fingers.

patent – able to be seen easily

Molded fingerprints are also easy to see. These prints are pressed into mud, wax, blood, or other soft materials.

molded – pressed into shape

Most prints at crime scenes cannot be seen easily. **Latent** fingerprints are left by body oil and sweat on the hands. Police spread powder over surfaces to find these fingerprints.

latent – hidden from sight

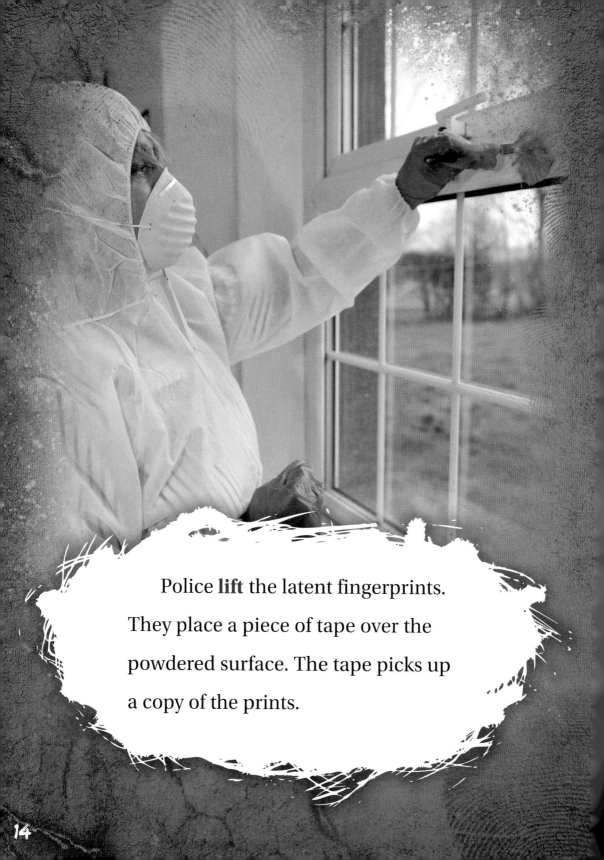

Police **lift** the latent fingerprints. They place a piece of tape over the powdered surface. The tape picks up a copy of the prints.

BLAZERS FACT

Investigators sometimes use powerful beams of light called lasers to spot latent fingerprints.

lift – to make a copy of a fingerprint from a surface

CHAPTER THREE

IN THE LAB

Police take the pictures and lifted prints to the crime lab. Fingerprint experts study the pattern of **ridges** on the prints. Loops, **whorls**, and arches are the basic patterns.

FINGERPRINT PATTERNS

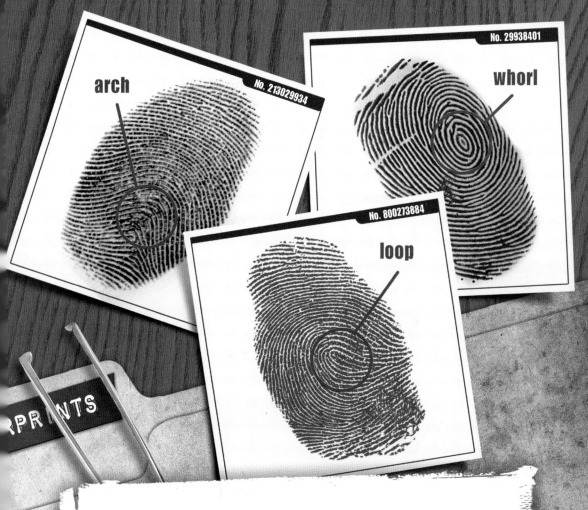

arch — No. 213029934

whorl — No. 29938401

loop — No. 800273884

RPRINTS

ridge – a raised area of skin on a fingertip

whorl – a pattern in which the ridges form at least one complete circle

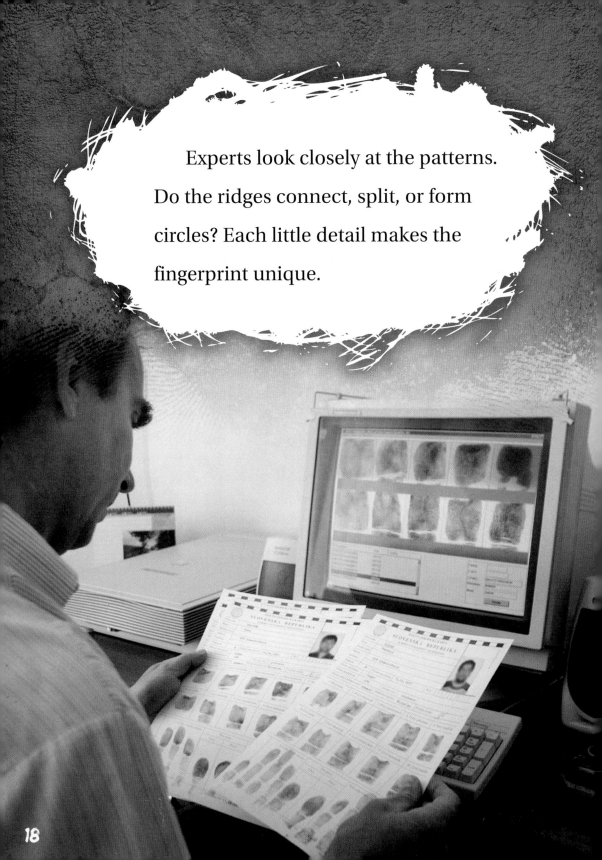

Experts look closely at the patterns. Do the ridges connect, split, or form circles? Each little detail makes the fingerprint unique.

BLAZERS FACT

Loops are the most common fingerprint pattern.

Sometimes police have a **suspect** in mind. An expert compares the suspect's prints to those from the crime scene. If the prints match, the suspect is arrested.

suspect – someone who may be responsible for a crime

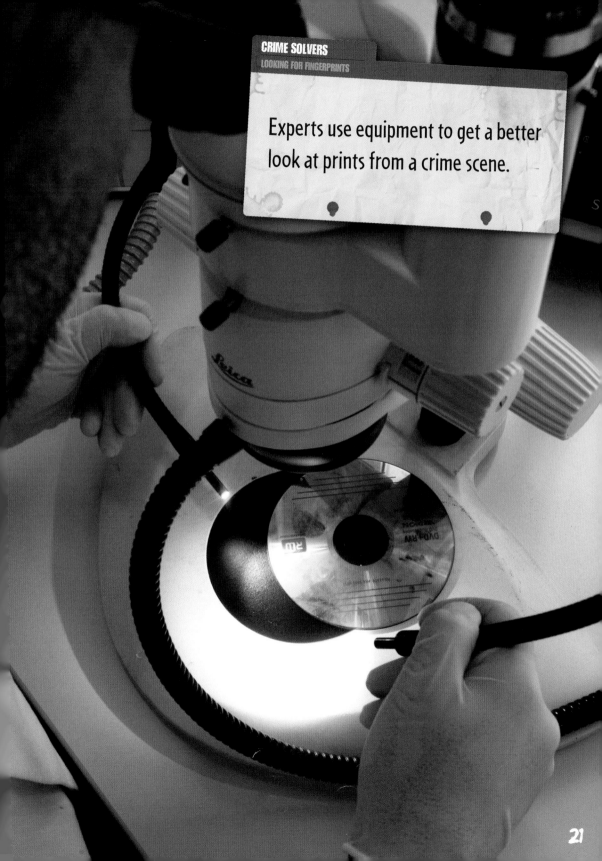

Experts use equipment to get a better look at prints from a crime scene.

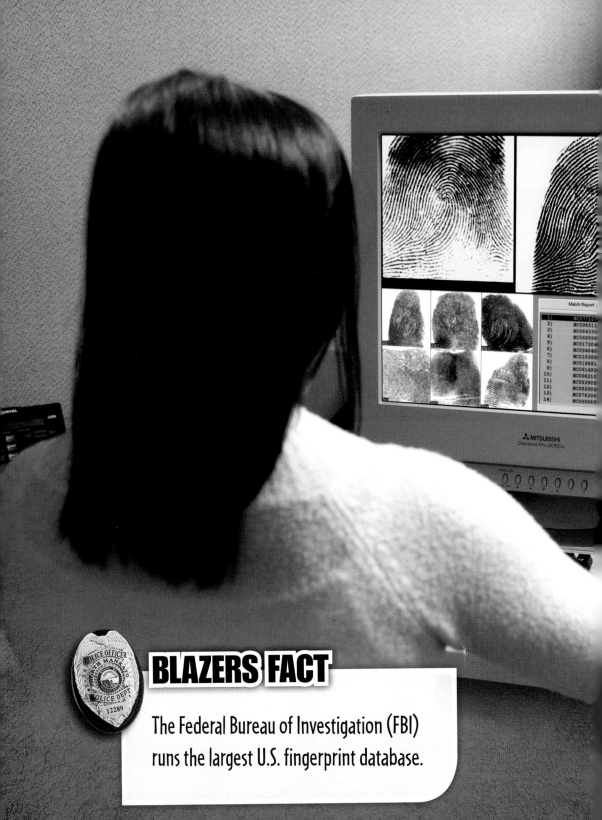

BLAZERS FACT

The Federal Bureau of Investigation (FBI) runs the largest U.S. fingerprint database.

If there is no suspect, police run prints through a **database**. This system stores millions of recorded prints. The system can find possible matches after about two hours.

database – information that is organized and stored in a central location

BLAZERS FACT

Fingerprints are formed before you are born. They do not change as you get older.

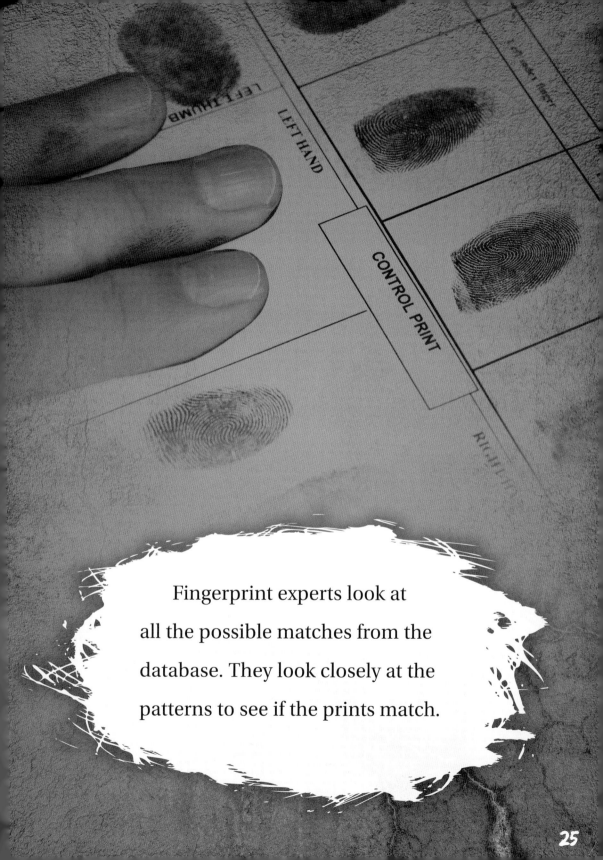

Fingerprint experts look at all the possible matches from the database. They look closely at the patterns to see if the prints match.

CHAPTER FOUR

MAKING THE CASE

Police have used fingerprints to solve crimes since the early 1900s. Police often use fingerprints to link someone to a crime.

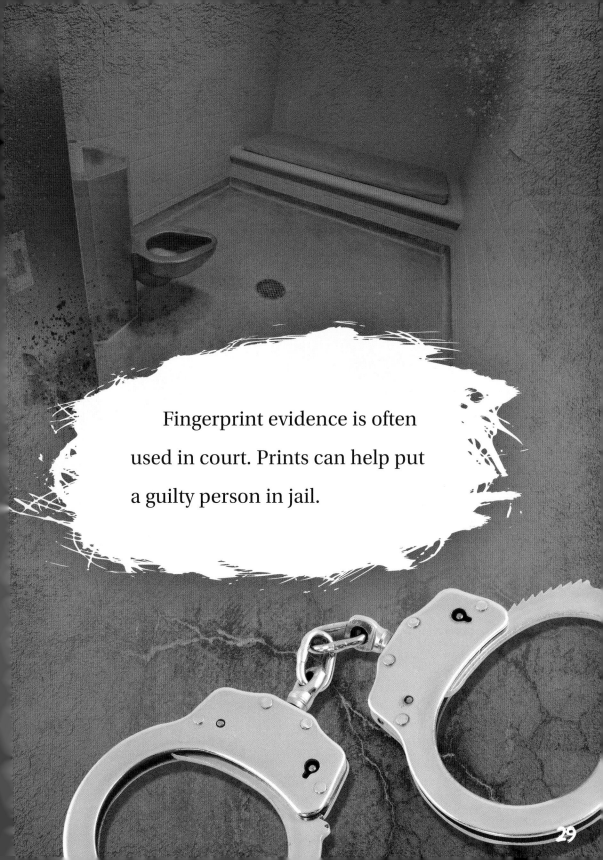

Fingerprint evidence is often used in court. Prints can help put a guilty person in jail.

Glossary

criminal (KRI-muh-nuhl) — someone who commits a crime

database (DAY-tuh-bays) — information that is organized and stored in a central location; most fingerprint records are stored in a computer database.

latent (LAY-tuhnt) — hidden from sight; latent fingerprints need to be developed to be seen.

lift (LIFT) — to copy a fingerprint from a surface

molded (MOHLD-id) — pressed into shape

patent (PAT-uhnt) — able to be seen with the naked eye; people can see patent fingerprints without developing them.

ridge (RIJ) — a raised area of skin on a fingertip

suspect (SUHSS-pekt) — someone who may be responsible for a crime

whorl (HORL) — a fingerprint pattern in which ridges form at least one complete circle

Read More

Beres, D. B. *Dusted and Busted!: The Science of Fingerprinting.* 24/7: Science behind the Scenes. New York: Franklin Watts, 2007.

Hamilton, Sue. *Fingerprint Analysis: Hints from Prints.* Crime Scene Investigation. Edina, Minn.: ABDO, 2008.

Scott, Carey. *Crime Scene Detective: Become a Forensics Super Sleuth, with Do-It-Yourself Activities.* New York: DK, 2007.

Internet Sites

FactHound offers a safe, fun way to find Internet sites related to this book. All of the sites on FactHound have been researched by our staff.

Here's all you do:

Visit *www.facthound.com*

FactHound will fetch the best sites for you!

Index

12/09

mL